BOOK III

CAPTAIN WORTHY'S WARSHIP ADVENTURES

WILLIAM MILBORN

authorHOUSE®

AuthorHouse™
1663 Liberty Drive
Bloomington, IN 47403
www.authorhouse.com
Phone: 1 (800) 839-8640

© 2019 William Milborn. All rights reserved.

No part of this book may be reproduced, stored in a retrieval system, or transmitted by any means without the written permission of the author.

Published by AuthorHouse 05/11/2019

ISBN: 978-1-7283-1182-1 (sc)
ISBN: 978-1-7283-1181-4 (e)

Print information available on the last page.

Any people depicted in stock imagery provided by Getty Images are models, and such images are being used for illustrative purposes only.
Certain stock imagery © Getty Images.

This book is printed on acid-free paper.

Because of the dynamic nature of the Internet, any web addresses or links contained in this book may have changed since publication and may no longer be valid. The views expressed in this work are solely those of the author and do not necessarily reflect the views of the publisher, and the publisher hereby disclaims any responsibility for them.

We were so anxious to set about on our journey that I thought that loading the ship would never end. But we must not forget a thing, for we knew not what our adventures might bring. I made sure that Captain John's Master Cannoneers and my Master Cannoneers had an ample amount of firepower to put down any enemy ships that we might confront or one that we just might like to commandeer. Finally, Captain O'Day, of the merchant ship, signaled that he was ready. Captain John also signaled he was ready. Then I pronounced those magic words, "untie from the mooring and weight anchor!"

I called out, "Half-sail and trim!" and we ever so slowly turned into the harbor. I said, "Will and Annabelle, I feel that this is the worst of a day for me as I leave my beloved Cuba! But it is the best day for us as we face the excitement of the future adventures awaiting!" We slowly left the port and turned westward on the sea. It was then that I saw the shore lined with cabins waving all along the way. I heard ten cannoneers salute to us in honor of what we had done for Cuba and its people. Annabelle even cried. Will was just excited and I had to stay my emotions. We were in no hurry so I maintained half-sail taking in the beauty of the northern shore of Cuba.

Soon Cuba was nearly out of sight when I felt Annabelle tugging on my arm. I said, "What?" She replied, "I have a secret to tell you." I said, "Annabelle, another child?" She said, "Oh no, not yet!" "Well what I asked." Then I heard her secret. She looked at me and said, "MY love, I was born lifeless." I was stunned. She said, "Yes, my Captain, I was not breathing. No matter how hard they tried. Then I suddenly took a quick breath of air. I was alive. My mother and father said it was an "Irish Miracle" of an angel that brought me to life. He then wanted to call me Angel and they did for a few months until the Catholic Priest said it would be best if I had another name. The priest told us a number of reasons why. So, I was given a first name of Annabelle, honoring my Mother Anne and a middle name of Angel!"

I said, "Remarkable! Had I known that I would have put 'Angel' in gold on the side of my ship. It is still not a bad idea. I will think on that."

Annabelle said, "That, my love, is my secret." That gave me something to think about for a while. Should I call you Annabelle Worthy or Angel Worthy? What do you think Will? You heard the story.

His response was interesting. He said, "I don't know. I think, if you don't mind, may I just call her Mother!" I said, "Absolutely!" The dilemma still existed, but in private I will call her Angel and among the officers and crewmen she will still be Annabelle. After all that is a powerful name on the side of the ship----known by many! I wondered why Annabelle chose to tell me her secret. Was there a message that I was not understanding?

The navigator set course for Jamaica to pick up as much rum as we could carry for that is what we will barter with along the way when we turn west again! We moved slowly---It was a beautiful night!

I had my lieutenant and Captain John's lieutenant board skiffs and go directly to the mooring docks. I gave my word in writing that we would buy all the containers of Jamaican rum available including flasks, bottles and cannisters and bring them to the mooring dock. We will anchor in the middle of Montigo Bay and wait. Soon we saw one of their boats come directly to my ships and they said in a Jamaican accent, "This is a test---We have ten barrels of Jamaican Rum. Pay us twenty-five pieces of silver and we will see if you truly have the wealth to buy all the rum you can come by."

I said, "Lieutenant, go to our coffers and weight out twenty-five pieces of silver plus two gold coins and pass it by box down to the Jamaican boat!" The Jamaican officer said, "We will make the deal! Where do you want me to put the barrels?" I said, "Sail your boat to the side of the merchant ship. They will tie onto the barrels and bring them on board."

I then said to their captain, "After you have done so, we will wait until the mooring dock is stacked with all the containers of rum that you can beg, borrow or steal. One-by-one my ships will sidle up to your mooring dock where you can load the rum onto our ships. Determine what your price will be! I will expect a discount if you want further purchases. I will pay directly on the spot in a strong box of silver plus a few gold pieces. If your price is higher than the value of the silver

We were elated that we were achieving our objective. I had no idea how much we had bought or how much we had spent! We were no longer at anchor and now under 'soft-sail' and what should happen? The best laid plans always seem to go awry! As we were ready to leave Montigo Bay, a massive four-masted pirate ship came speeding toward us in full-sail. Somehow it had learned that we were giving out massive amounts of silver to the merchants for rum. I saw that it was meaning to do us harm, for its gun portals were open. I did not have to order my cannoneers to take position. To them it was automatic. I placed my ship in front of the merchant ship to protect it. I opened all eighty cannonballs on top of that pirate ship and their masts began crumbling. The crew was jumping over board as fire began erupting from our well-placed cannonballs. I ordered medium-sail, for our merchant ship could travel no faster and we circumnavigated that fiery grave of a pirate ship. We were relieved as we left Montigo Bay. The navigator adjusted direction. The sail-master adjusted sails, and once again we headed west.

You know I did not put my Angel and son Will at risk, for I had them hide away in the cabin which was steel plated. I expect that Mickey and Anne were also hiding in their cabin listening to the roar of cannons. I went to Mickey's cabin and knocked on the door. Micky O'Hara popped out and said, "Wow!" I looked at him and if ever I saw a man that was three sheets to the wind, it has he! I turned him around and gently pushed him back into his cabin and said, "Never fear Mickey, for I am here---you are okay! See you in the morning…"

It was the blackest of nights---no moon, no stars. There were a million fireflies all around and it was beautiful but dangerous for we could run aground with out any light at night. To the west we saw the faint gas lights of Cuba.

There were no signs of wind and the sounds could carry easily. I took the bull by the horn and called to Captain John on the other warship and said, "We are going to make for Cuba and anchor in the harbor. Within the hour under minimum-sail, we maneuvered our way back into the Cuban harbor from whence we had left. There was sufficient gas light from the city to allow us to maneuver into position for early morning departure. We dropped anchor. Everyone felt the need for some good sleep. Even Aaron's horses on the merchant ship were sleepy.

I automatically arose from my sleep when the slightest bit of light shown at dawn and lit up the sky. With a bull horn I told all passengers, "Prepare for sailing! Eat something! Drink something! And please attend to yourselves in other ways. We will raise anchor in one hour." And that we did! In exactly one hour we went to half-sail and used what little wind that there was to find our way out of the Cuban harbor into the Gulf of Mexico. I took the local merchant ship and Captain John's four-masted followed. We were an imposing threat to any pirate ship waiting in the gulf to make a kill. I hate to admit it but I am not a smooth water, gulf man, but rather an ocean man whose waters are high. The challenge of sailing in the precise direction I needed to go was simple.

My worry now was how to get to New Orleans on the Mississippi Delta. There were sand bars and little islands everywhere. When I arrived at a co-ordinate that I thought was a place to sail North, I was confused as to the safest way to navigate all of these Delta sand bars. I ordered that we all drop anchor but we were too deep in water for our anchors to hold bottom. So, we sailed out into the gulf and circled until we observed another large ship tracking its way North through a channel we could not see. I guessed it was bound for New Orleans at the mouth of the Big River. I directed our course to follow that ship. That ship's captain must have been in fear of capture by my two ships flying the "Jolly Rodgers"!

I quickly ordered that our "Jolly Rodger" flag be dropped and French flags be hoisted on all masts, because I knew the French had been exploring and claiming land in the Louisiana Territory and the Mississippi.

I am practically having to re-learn navigation in these quiet waters. Our warships were not designed to go at a snail's pace. Even under low-sail we were moving too fast through those Delta waters. Occasionally, I heard the scraping of my hull as I got too near a sand bar or small island. I could not maneuver under such low-sail.

I had an idea! On the fog horn I said, "Captain John, lower your anchor ten feet and wedge it in that position any way you can! Of course, my men heard the order and immediately lowered our iron bar and we dropped anchor one-fourth of the way down to keep it from going to the bottom. This slowed us down to the point where I could add more sails and have more control.

As we neared the entrance to the Mississippi River, there were more lights than I had seen since we left England. Shortly we found ourselves at the entrance to a massive New Orleans harbor. We could see ships flying flags from all nations.

I sent my First Lieutenant on the skiff to the harbor dock with a few gold coins and I said, "Find a place on the massive waterfront where we can moor our three ships together." The gold coins worked for within an hour Lieutenant Bannon arrived back to the ship with the skiff and said, "Sir, we have an outstanding mooring point on the docks. The gold helped." I said, "Lieutenant Bannon, you had better know where. Point the way!" He did his best but the harbor master was on shore waving a gas lantern and directing where I could dock and moor my ship. He did the same for my merchant ship and then Captain John's warship.

I saw no other four-masted ships in the harbor but there were three-masted ships and merchant ships aplenty. I said to the captain of the merchant ship, "We will now all meet on shore and I will give you further orders." All of the cannoneers, crewmen and seamen were elated. They felt like they were somehow home again. When everyone had assembled, I said, "Sit down and listen to what I have to say. It will take a spell!"

I began, "The people you will encounter are also adventurers. Among them there will be many thieves and gamblers. This is a primarily French part of the country so use a French accent if you can and learn a few French words. If you haven't done so already, talk to our teacher, the thin man. We will only be here as long as it takes to resupply our ships. You officers will help my lieutenants get this done quietly and efficiently. You will have an abundance of coin on you. Do not flash it for you might meet some evil-doers who might just 'do you in' for it. Go in threes and that means all of you seamen as well. You wouldn't be happy unless you explored the area so do so with much care and with your daggers available on your belts. In your groups of three, one of you should also carry a pistol in case you engage with those who would do you harm. Put a smile on your face, be friendly and laugh and join the dancing at the pubs. Do not come wobbling back to the ship drunk. You must be back on board this ship by eleven tonight. I expect you lieutenants and officers will have to rent or commandeer some wagons to store the ship with our needs during our trip north. You have only tomorrow to get it done for we leave the next morning when the rooster crows. If any crewmen or seamen does not follow my orders, I will leave them here without question because your future life could depend on your following my orders. You are in a new world, crewmen. You all have a pocket full of shilling to buy beer and other entertainment. Do not show one piece of silver or gold. Only my lieutenants and officers are allowed to carry that with them for purchasing for our trip. Keep your money in a small bag made of leather and hang it from our belt on the inside of your pants. We have those pouches with coin which we are filling for you as we speak. There are not so many coins in each pouch that they will be uncomfortable for you to carry as they hang next to your groin. Carry a few shillings in your pocket in case you become engaged with a thief. If that happens, just give them the coins from your pocket and let them go! Do not pick a fight or use your dagger or pistol unless absolutely necessary. I know you could 'do in' any one that accosts you, but you won't---do you hear me? I guess then I can say have a good time!"

"Mickey, Anne, Will and Aaron---you stay on board the ship, as I will. I want five of my warrior crewmen to stay aboard each ship with pistols loaded and be ready to put down any man that tries to board us. Warn anyone that comes near the ship that you will shoot them if they come near. You have valuables to protect. Now go about your business. If it is unclear what I have said, talk to your superior officers. Do not get yourselves killed but try to enjoy this French area. Do not bring back to the ship anything more than what you left with, except for your poker winnings."

Everyone was out doing what they wanted. Annabelle joined Mickey and Anne in their cabin. The warrior crewmen took their places on the deck as ordered. I sat down on the mooring post and started thinking about the trip up river. I must have started to doze while sitting up. When I became aware, I heard crying, screaming and yelling. I saw three of my crewmen approach me with blood on their faces, streaming down their faces and their arms. I asked, "Seamen, how bad are those injuries?"

They said, "Sir, most all of it are flesh wounds. Our pride is hurt worse than our bodies." I asked, "What happened men?" They said, "I thought we were having a friendly game of poker at a club called 'The Aces'.

They seemed friendly enough until Smitty won a big pot. They cried out, 'cheaters' and came at us tooth and nail with knives. You know we could have killed them, Captain!"

I said, "I know you could have. I also know you learned not to cheat for the penalty on board the ship is a meeting with the 'cat'. Men, we will not just abide with these men bragging to others about how they whipped, beat, defeated, and chased you back to the ship. That word would soon spread and damage our reputation. Direct the way crewmen. I will follow you to the 'Aces' pub and I will deal with this problem."

Within minutes we pushed through their swinging doors and entered. There were four men at the bar and three men at the poker table who had given my men a beating. Of course, like most cases, the mere sight of my demeanor of six foot six inches was intimidating. I had an edge to begin with. One of the men pointed his finger at me and said, "You had to bring your daddy with you, didn't you?" The minute that finger pointed at me I swung my epee underhanded and cut off the tip of his finger. The man tried to retrieve it as it fell to the floor. He ran howling out onto the street holding his hand and screaming HELP!

I yelled, "Don't worry. You will be okay! Do you other three have any inclination to defend your other poker friends? There are three of you and just one of me. My men could help, but I won't let them kill the likes of you. They have my orders not to do so or they would have killed your poker playing friends."

One of the largest of the men at the bar said, "In that case we will just have to shoot you and put our daggers to you!" At that very instant with another swift movement I cut his ear off. As soon as I sliced his ear off, I reached for his bloody ear and gave it back to him. He ran from the place screaming.

I said to the man standing at the bar, "Are you still brave enough to pull your pistol? All I have is my epee." I could not believe that he would still pull a pistol with the intent of killing me. Before he could cock it, I came down on his pistol and I cut and broke all of his fingers. His gun fell to the floor. He too, went screaming from the place leaving a trail of blood. I said to the fourth man, "Your friends will think you are a coward if you leave without some injury. Now, where would you like it and what would you like?" He said, "Sir, can I think on that?" I said, "No, I think not. Turn around or you will die!" He turned around and I took a small bit of his scalp from his head with my epee. I slashed a bit of scalp from the back of his head. I said, "Here, take your scalp back with you so you can brag about your fight!" He held his hairy scalp over the back of his head and scurried out leaving a trail of blood. He left screaming and crying all the way just like a baby.

I turned to my three injured seamen and said, "No one has to die! I think the word will be spreading quickly not to mess with any seamen from our ship." They were in absolute awe. The three gamblers sat in their chairs without moving. They were afraid to say or do anything. I glowered at them. I said, "What should I do with coward cheaters?" One of them said, "We did not cheat you. You just claimed that we did." I replied, "None of my men cheat for fear of the 'cat-of-nine-tails'!" I then said, "What to do with you? Take your decks of cards from your persons and lay the decks on the table. Put them nice and even---side-by-side on the table. Spread them further apart please." They did so immediately. I said, "Your kind of decks are hard to come by!" I drew my sword from its sheath and cut them down the middle. I said, "Gentlemen, you might say I just 'cut' the deck for the next round of poker, which you may never play!"

The men were sweating profusely. I said, "I am going to let you off easy. Place every bit of money you have on the middle of the table---Both your money and the money you have taken from my seamen. Now, lets have some jewelry. Take your earrings out, give me your watches and pull off those diamond and ruby rings on your fingers and put them in the center of the table. Place all of your guns, daggers and knives on the table as well. Also empty your pockets so that I may see. Seamen pick up all of that booty. Wrap it all in this tablecloth and split it when you get back to the ship. But no---that doesn't seem fair does it? Before you take the booty, leave it on the table and we will play 'high-low' for all that is on the table." The gambler said, "You probably know where all the winning cards are—don't you?"

I said, "No, lets watch you shuffle the deck. Now hold all these cards face down to you. I will hold the deck and fan the cards out. You pick one from the deck and I will pick one also. In fact, I will pick first." I reached and drew forth my card. I looked at it and I showed them a three of hearts. I said, "Well, it looks like you may win after all!" I showed them my three of hearts and they all grinned and said, "which one of you will pick the winner?" The grizzly one said, "I'll do it!" I spread the cards for him to pick. He looked and grabbed one from the center of the deck. He drew it forth and held it to the light---it was the deuce of spades. The poker boys said in unison, "Damn!" I looked at them and said, "I have taken everything that you apparently have so before you leave, if you promise you will never again cheat at poker, I will give you each a silver coin. These silver coins are worth more than anything on this table. Do I have your word?" They said, "Yeah, we are grateful that you have given us a new life!"

I said to my seamen, "Gather your booty up---it is all yours! Let's go to the ship. One of my seamen looked at me and said, "How…? How…? How…?" I said, "That's a trade secret!"

When I cut that deck a time or two,

I saw the deuce. I than put the back half of the deck on top and kept a finger where the deuce was. I covered that with my right hand and spread the cards and while he was starring and grinning at me, which he was the whole time, I then reached towards the middle of the deck and pushed that deuce out slightly further than the rest of the cards. As he picked the card, I pushed the deuce out even further and he took it!

See, even your captain can cheat, but its okay to cheat a cheater. You may speak of this episode except for the cheating. If I hear about that, the 'cats' going to take a bite out of your behinds. I never saw three happier seamen as they galloped back to the Annabelle.

I too, retired to my ship. I entered my cabin and for the first time I can recall, I laid myself down in full uniform. I re-thought what had recently transpired in that pub, and how I had put my life in jeopardy. I thought…"Not good!...Not wise!..."

Early in the morning, Captain John rapped on my cabin door. I said, "Come!" He entered with a deep frown on his face. I knew that he knew and I said, "I won't put my life in jeopardy again as I did last night." Captain John said, "Thank you Sir, I want to report to you that throughout the night and this morning the ships were fully loaded. It was quite a thing to see as everyone speedily loaded our ships for the trip north on the Big River. I checked with the loading captains and they said that our inventory showed we were overloaded. This was in part my fault Sir, for I had purchased saddles for all of the horses and buggies and wagons with their parts to be assembled later." I said, "Captain John, good thinking! Congratulations! Now please assemble all crewmen, seamen and officers on the decks. I must speak to them from my place at the helm of the Annabelle." Captain John immediately left to see to it that my orders were complied with.

When all were assembled and all were looking up at me at the helm I said, "I know by now that you know what I did at that pub called 'The Aces'. I did that so the word would spread along the docks that my crewmen would not be considered weak or not supported. That unfortunately would cause others to think that they could easily confront us and damage or hurt us. The three crewmen that were cheated at cards, by now, have told the story and probably have enhanced it. I did not come to their aide for that singular purpose of protecting my crewmen but, rather to protect the image of all crewmen visiting this port."

I said, "You are thinking why does it matter since we are now leaving? Well gentlemen, it matters to me! As I dwell on the last evening, I feel I could have made a mistake in placing my life as your leader at stake. That was a mistake. It all depends on how you wish to see it. I must tell you one thing and that is I have no favorites among you, including the three from last night. You are all equal in my estimation. I have not a friend or buddy among you and I want it kept that way. Do not approach me on any matter. Speak to your officers in charge of you and they will in time speak to their lieutenants to whom they report and the lieutenant will speak to me. There are three of you still laying in your quarters with the whiskey disease and unable to be with us. They will not receive the "cat-of-nine-tails", but the "cat-of-three-tails" will leave a reminder on their behinds for what they have done. We have one crewman that has disappeared. I warned you! Now, we are going to weight anchor." Just as we had weighed anchor and were moving gently into the bay, I saw our lost crewman running like the wind to get aboard. He made a gigantic long leap at the end of the dock and caught the rope ladder then climbed aboard. I yelled at him, "You get the 'cat' you know!" He said, "I know!"

I was not so fortunate to get out of the New Orleans Bay without interference, for there were three pirate ships with their "Jolly Rodgers" hanging high. There was one two-masted and two three-masted pirate ships blocking our way to the river. Apparently, they got word of the amount of silver and gold we were spending to load our three ships with stores. Being the pirates that they were, they could not leave with the thought of missing a possible windfall of treasure. I thought, "What a surprise they have in store!"

I placed the bow of my ship facing the three pirate ships and said, "Fire cannoneers…fire!" With the long cannons, we could reach their ships. Immediately you could see the cannonballs ripping into the center of the first ship's deck. No sooner than the cannonballs struck, my cannoneers reloaded and sent another volley to the second ship. It hit low, just below their deck and hit their magazine of powder and that ship blew into fragments. The fire shot high and lit up the whole entry to the bay. I said, "Gunmen, you are lucky. Try to bounce a couple cannonballs into the mast of that third pirate ship with its "Jolly Rodgers" flying.

I knew Captain John of my other warship marveled at what my cannoneers had done with my long cannons. He was happy enough not to engage in battle. My cannoneers weren't so lucky but they did manage to tear up the deck of that third ship. They still had cannon fire that could do us damage. I said, "No problem! cannoneers, continue with practicing your cannon fire until you put down that third ship. By the way, put another round of fire into that first ship." Indeed, that first ship had turned sideways to us and was sending cannon fire towards us.

The cannon fire from the three-masted ship was landing too close to the Annabelle. My merchant ship with Aaron's horses had drifted somewhat out into the bay. Suddenly, there was a blast from the enemy cannons that hit our merchant ship and the horses' stalls. I heard a horrible sounding whining as one of the poor thoroughbreds fell. I said, "Oh no! Cannoneers, give them all of your fire power. Fire forty cannonballs and disassemble that ship." Captain John saw what I was doing and he managed to turn his ship sideways so his cannons could fire onto the enemy ship. He fired forty more shots into that first ship. I yelled, "Cease fire!" So did Captain John. That display will certainly give second thoughts to ay other ship on the northern bay that might accost us. The bay was full of debris and screaming seamen, so I ordered to re-anchor in place until the next morning.

I arose to see other small boats at the entrance to the bay. They were clearing a way to the entrance so that they could depart. Again, I said, "Weigh anchor! I want us at half-sail and we will move west to the Big River." We cleared that entry where we could see dead seamen floating.

We pressed our way through the debris and finally knew that my three ships would be heading north up this magnificent river.

Just as I said, "Weigh anchor", Aaron called to me with the bull horn, "My good sir, the enemy has killed one of my thoroughbreds name 'Whiskers'. He reached his life's end by a pirate's cannonball." I said, "Just as soon as we get to the Mississippi, we will have a burial at sea for your horse. Be ready to say a few words. Make it look the best you can and come up with a way that you can lay that horse on a plank that can be tilted to give it a burial." I thought to myself, "I have never heard of a burial at sea for a horse!" I said to Captain John, "We will now endeavor to put the horse's hind section on the plank and let him slide into the water." I observed that Aaron was crying at losing this thoroughbred as he helped lift the plank and let his horse slide into the river.

Our ships were not moving at this point in honor of the burial of the horse. Our final thought was a sad one, as we looked down at "Whisker" floating in the water. The horse would not sink.

I said, "Sails up please. Give me a three-quarter sail and everybody try to stay together as we try to sail north. At some points the river was wide and at some points the river was narrow. It was those places we saw pioneers trying to float their wagons across the river and swim the horses across as well. There were camps all the way along the eastern side of the river comprised of wagons and horses and families with camp fires burning. I wondered if they were all trying to decide if they were going to continue westward. The pioneers on the eastern shore were all wondering how they were going to cross the Mississippi to go west.

We were moving slowly up this muddy river. It suddenly came to my mind, "Where am I going and why?" I thought that this is what I dreamed of doing long ago. That is to go inland, buy land and farm and raise my family with few worries since I had more money than I probably would ever need. But now as I come closer to realizing that old dream, I have become aware that this is not what I want to do. I

called to Captain John, "Pull over to the shore and weight anchor." And so, he did, along with the merchant ship. I followed in closely to them. There was no worry about ocean waves causing us to run aground or into each other.
I called out to John and Aaron, "Bring your families aboard the skiff to the Annabelle. All seamen aboard all ships come to the top deck where you will receive further orders." Soon everyone was there crowing around my cabin. I told them to sit on the deck for we would be there awhile. The first words I said were, "Captain John, do you wish to be a farmer?" He answered, "Hell no!" I said, "How does your family feel about that Captain John?" He said, "They are with me Sir!"

"Mickey and Anne O'Hara, do you wish to be farmers?" Mickey said, "Too old for that son! I said, "How does Anne O'Hara feel about that?" She said, "I had enough of that when I was a young girl in Ireland several years ago. My answer is no!"

"I know you Aaron. You want to be a horse rancher and breeder and race and sell horses! You don't care where. Is that right Aaron O'Hara!" He said, "Yes Captain."

I looked at Annabelle's face and said, "We have talked of this so long… having heard all the rest of the family, are you willing to give up our dreams of owning a farm?" Annabelle said, "My Captain, I thought that was your dream. What is your plan now?"

I gave directions to my other two officers on my ships, "Bring out a barrel of rum and drink while I sit and ponder over this dilemma. I went to the helm and by bull horn I said, "Captain John, seamen and officers---How many of you wish to be farmers?" They all said, "No… farming, No…fishing!" The officers of Captain John's ship said, "You men all have special skills in manning your warship as do mine. They want to continue to be your crewmen."

I called again, "Ask Captain John if his seamen would like to take jobs as fishermen on the boats on this river and make a living in such a manner?" He said, "Only three, Sir." I asked the same question of my men on the Annabelle and the merchant ship... "Only one, Sir...wait, there are two!"

"Mr. Booker T. T. Masters, my protector and teacher, I failed to ask you---Did you want to farm or fish?" It was the same question I asked the others. My tall, thin man responded, "If you want to be a farmer, I will plow the fields along with you, or we may plow through the turbulent seas!"

Mr. T. you have been my shadow for ever so long and have given me a sense of comfort. Your many skills with the arms of combat, as you promised, have been there for me to protect Annabelle, my son Will and myself. You are a part of my family. If you would allow her, Annabelle would help you meet a number of women that you might like to consider wedding and make a bunch of children just like you. Would you consider that? Booker responded, "I think not, Sir!" I said, "Alright, but keep in mind that the future may cause you to rethink your response!"

I said, "Thank you. Everyone, relax for now. Your orders will come later." I pulled my Captain's chair out of the cabin and sat there for the longest time. I pondered the alternatives. I must have had one hundred fifty people on those three ships that I would be making decisions for. I said, "Lieutenant, would you top off stein of rum and please have the same offered to everyone else. We will be here for a while."

Here I sat on the best four-masted warship in the world on this old Mississippi River. It was both sad and laughable in that I put so many people in jeopardy. After a few more swigs of grog, I called out on the bull horn, "There is one thing I wish to make very clear...Our children must have access to education and medical care and stable homes. I am now asking officers to take a tally of how many seamen have family and how many school age children?" I waited. "I want the same information from you officer O'Day." It was about an hour before I had the numbers in hand.

I thought and then asked them, "Where are your children and families?......Cuba, England, Ireland? As soon as I had that information, Captain John and I studied the results of that data and found that in all there were seventy-five (including my own officers and men) that had families and children. Ten families were in Cuba, fifteen in Ireland and the rest were in England. My son Will said, "Father, you have told me that I will be the fifth generation Captain of a Warship." I said, "That you will be my son." I announced loudly by bull horn to all aboard these ships that we were going back from whence we came."

I said, "We are still going to have some adventures before we make that return trip. We are going into the St. Louis port with our warship... the only water deep enough to accommodate our ship. We will anchor and spend two days to enjoy St. Louis. It is more sophisticated and I have been told has less crime. Dress as you choose, but mostly ordinary folks are wearing western type clothing...boots, belts, denim pants and wool shirts. They may have gun holders...more for 'show' than 'go'. I love their broad-brimmed, stetson hats. Weigh anchor and direct our warships towards the lights of St. Louis."

It was easy to see because St. Louis was the largest and most exotic city on the East bank of the Mississippi. With bull horn in hand I announced that we go directly to the open spaces of the dock. The water was deep enough there. I said, "I want ten warrior seamen at the edge of each warship with weapons in hand. You may not go ashore, but you will be relieved in ten hours by the warship warriors that were first to go ashore. One officer will stay aboard until he is relieved by a fellow officer in ten hours, when he returns to take his position. Everyone, this is to be your big adventure. Make the most of it in these two days. Don't get yourselves jailed by some stupid thing, or lose your money to thieves or get murdered. We will leave this coming Sunday at dawn!"

I said, "Let's go! Point the ships ahead. Anchors away! Every seaman is to have a silver coin and a pocket full of shillings. I will also give each of you one silver coin to buy your family something. We will find room for these things on board our ships. That goes for everyone! Aaron, I know where you are going. You are going to the Saddle shop. I know you want bridles and additional saddles, horse blankets and saddle bags as well. I will give you extra coins to rent a wagon so you may haul all that back to the merchant ship. Oh yes, you may hide away that silver coin to buy your family and Ida Lee some special things. Don't forget it, or I, as Captain, will make you pay!"

It was a thrill for all when we returned to the St. Louis harbor. The harbor was massive and just like New Orleans, there were ships there from all nations…bartering and doing business. I sent Lieutenant Harris by skiff with coin to see to it that the Harbor Master would clear enough dock frontage to accommodate our three ships.

Officer Harris reported that when the Dock Master saw the massive warship, he quickly made arrangements for some of the ships to clear out and make room for us to dock. I gave officer Harris sufficient coin to make that happen.

Within twenty minutes I had three ships sidled up next to the St. Louis dock with prime positioning for easy departure. We moored and everyone knew what they could not do and what they should do. We could not leave the ship fast enough to go to all the lighted entertainment and store fronts.

Our wives were beguiled as they saw Parisian salons and boutiques that were beckoning them to come in and buy. They headed that way of course. I had them accompanied by one of my warrior seamen. I gave them additional coin for what I know to be expensive women's clothing. More seamen hired a large carriage and placed it out front of the salon and stood before the horse that drove it. I since have discovered that they bought fancy under cloths, fancy gowns, and dresses of kinds that included female apparel like hats that could make them stand out at the most luxurious affairs back in London Town or anywhere else. I left them on that glorious venture while Captain John and I visited the western wear shops.

I bought some fancy western boots with two-inch heels and spurs and a pair of pants of some material that was new to me. I bought several western long sleeve cotton and wool shirts and a vest to hold my pocket watch and fob. I bought a couple of bandanas for around my neck and two Stetson hats, one black and one tan. Then I said, "Storekeeper, double that order. Captain John, you double your order as well and I will pay for all of it!" Captain John said, "Let's you and I just put on an outfit each, and dress in full attire in our cowboy outfits and hit the street as bonified "dressed' cowboys. Oh, and storekeeper, I want what we just bought in junior sizes for our sons." He was getting it all together and priced while Captain John and I transformed ourselves into all-American cowboys.

I will give extra coin to deliver this order to my warship the Annabelle. An officer will be waiting for you to give him this note. Deliver Captain John's order to his warship the Neptune as well. I have payed you plenty, I know. What I have payed you, you are to keep for yourself and not say a word to anyone. Oh my God, we both have to have those gun belts and those shiny pearl handled pistols. Those are just for ourselves, not our sons." Within ten to fifteen minutes Captain John and I were dressed the part and had strapped on a gun belt and holsters with western guns.

I said, "Captain John, I must tell you I am going to strap on my epee too. I feel weakened without having my epee strapped to my left hip." John said, "No problem, Sir!" We doffed our Stetsons to the storekeeper and told him we would send him more business. I said, "I am sure our lieutenants and officers would like this attire as well."

We stepped out of the western wear store and everyone along the street stopped and looked at us and I said, "Captain John, do you think we have overdone it?" He said, "Whatever makes us happy!" I knew that my six-foot six-inch height had become six-foot eight-inches with the high heels on the boots I just bought. That alone, considering my broad shoulders, would bring attention from almost anyone.

The storekeeper said that this was the largest size order of western wear he had ever sold. I am glad he had it. Captain John had seen other cowboys walk with a bowlegged strut, so we fashioned our own walk to look similar. It wasn't more than ten minutes later when several real cowboys left the swinging doors of a real western saloon.

They quickly stopped and stared at us. The biggest cowboy always has the biggest mouth and he said, "Ho…Ho…Ho…! Are you the cow or are you the boy?" He was within three or four feet of me and I said, "Very funny my friend, I am the bull!" Then I unleashed my epee with a quick motion and severed his gun strap. It fell to the ground.

His friends, of which there were several, stepped around to take a closer look at us and said, "Wow, Mr. Big Man, we were only joshing you. We meant no harm. We were just out for a good time. Come back into the saloon and we will have a friendly drink." I said, "Fine, I will even buy! It's on me! Whatever you want!" The boys bought the biggest and best drinks that the saloon had to offer and said, "Thank you cowboy!" Those were good words that Captain John and I wanted to hear. I said, "Here's a few shillings to have a round on me. When you see more cowboys come that are not from here, they are only trying to see what it feels like to wear western clothes. Under those cowboy outfits are highly trained killers. They are men of the sea that man the four-masted warship called the Annabelle. Please spread the word to everyone you see that we want to be friends. The crew want to enjoy your town and take in the sights…the women as well. Be kind to them all and we will treat you the same." I continued, "With our cannons, we could bring down the whole waterfront in minutes. Why would we? If we do, it is because western heathens think they have something to gain by looting and attacking us." After that conversation, Captain John and I went strutting down the boardwalk doing our best to look like and be like bonified cowboys.

We rattled our spurs a time or two, and walked to the end of that long, long St. Louis boardwalk. We both were tempted to step into one of the dance halls featuring can-can dances. Alone we may have entered, but together we would know of each other's indiscretions. So, we chose not to, but we took a peek into these places anyway. We saw our crewmen bobbing in and out of these fun places. Some looked at us like they knew us but didn't believe it was us since we were dressed in western clothes.

Just as we were about to turn back to our ships, we came across a few men that were bent on paying us a visit. They were not dressed as cowboys. They came out of the darkness. It was easy to see they were hoodlums bent on thievery.

The minute they slipped into the light, I drew my epee and gave a single slash to the faces of the first two men I encountered. Then with my western gun, I put a bullet in the hand of the third man. Captain John readily took care of the other two as he put bullets into their groins. I said, "Captain John, you are a hateful person." We laughed and I said, "Just like on the high seas. Captain John, why do people want to hurt us? Is it because we look like we have money? What do you think?"

As we turned and walked away to our ship, I heard the screaming, crying and yelling of the would-be thieves...off to lick their wounds! Who knows...We may have turned their lives around. We certainly changed their appearance!

On the way back we passed the saloon where we had made friends with the cowboys that we bought drinks for. They were standing outside the saloon. One of them was carrying his gun belt over his shoulder for I had destroyed it with my epee. I walked up close to them and pressed a silver coin into his palm and whispered, "Don't tell anyone, but I want you to buy a new gun belt and holster and two of the best new western guns you can buy. Do this when you are not around your friends so that they will not know where and how you now own the best western guns, belts, and pistols on the dock. I ask you one thing…I do not need to know your name, but I ask you to be a kind and gentle man. Will you promise that to me?" He said, "Yes Sir!" I said, "And control your friends as well. Find other ways to have fun rather than to intimidate strangers."

I felt good about that as Captain John and I strolled to the other end of the wide boardwalk. He and I walked that boardwalk till nearly dawn observing and making small talk. We noticed all of the wagons and knew that their owners were worrying as to how they were going to move their wagons and supplies and pioneer families across the Mississippi River.

On the way back to our individual ships, we saw a man standing and looking at the Mississippi. I stopped and said, "I know what you are wondering. Here is y response…Gather a group of your fellow pioneers. Al of you pool enough money to rent or buy a barge. Pull it to shore and make a big gate and ramp so that gradually a few horses and wagons (just a few at a time) may cross this river. The man said, "Yes…Yes I will…!" Captain John looked at me and shook his head and said, "Captain Joseph, Sir, you are a wonder!"

As we neared our ships and Captain John went to his warship and I to my Annabelle, I said, "Captain John, this evening was a treat!" Captain john responded, "Aye, Sir, it certainly was!"

I slept most of the morning and rose too late in the day. It is something a captain should never do. I packed away my cowboy duds and pistols but kept my Stetson out to wear as I pleased. I wouldn't be much of a captain if I didn't have several scouts out bringing news from all three ships.

Our wives had brought back some things for we husbands. The captain's wife from the merchant ship had brought her husband a spy glass. It was something he coveted but did not own. Ida Lee brought Aaron a cowboy hat, shirt, and vest and a new pair of boots. She said, "Here's a large box of sugar cubes you can use to treat your thoroughbreds." Captain John's wife, Lisa, bought everything she needed and Captain John bought everything he needed. Lisa bought him a grand surprise though. It was a gift of a gold pocket watch and fob that he always wanted. Ida Lee approached Aaron and said, "I have something special to give to you but not right at the moment." He asked his wife, "What is it?" She said, "It was a secret, but, oh well…You will soon know that secret anyway. I am making a third child for you!" He screamed with delight, "You make me happier than ever before!"

My Annabelle came over to me and said, "I don't expect anything more because I bought everything I needed and so did you. But I could not resist…I want you to open this felt box." I did and there were two beautiful pipes. One was straight and the other one curved down and then up like a horn. They were made of rosewood and brandished with mother-of-pearl stems. I could not believe I now had something I wanted that I didn't have to pay for myself. Annabelle said, "My Captain, the pipes will not do you any good without this." She brought forth another box wherein there were packages of all kinds of tobacco. Right then and there I pulled out the pipe and loaded it with Cuban tobacco. I pressed the tobacco into the pipe and lit it and drew several times so the tobacco was burning and emitting a wonderful aroma. Now, I could draw smoke through the rosewood stem. The taste was wonderful. I sat in my Captain's chair and said, "Thank you Annabelle. You can leave me to savor the luxury of your gift!!" Then she went about doing her routine tasks.

My scout returned and said, "Captain, I don't think St. Louis has any more Parisian underclothing. It has been bought by crewmen and officers as gifts to their wives when they return home." I said, "Do you think they bought all the lingerie for their loved ones or do you think they bought it for them to enjoy seeing it on their women?" "Both Sir... both. I believe both!" "Good job crewman and I flipped him a shilling."

I went to Booker T. T. Masters' cabin and there I saw my tall, thin man squatting by his bed surrounded by dozens of books. Booker smiled at me and said, "Look what I found. Look at all these books that were for sale by authors from everywhere. Sir, I am reading one now by Thomas Payne...A man I would love to meet." I said, "Wonderful Mr. T. I will leave you to your pleasure. I have Captain's duties to get along with."

Even my crewmen, with heavy heads, managed to get all the ships loaded for our voyage. Officers were even sweating as they loaded barrels of water, smoked meats, and bags of flour, sugar, potatoes and all sorts of beans. They loaded several cases of honey and jam. Now that was something new. They loaded cases of eggs, pounds and pounds of bacon which was to be the first to be eaten. There was rye, oats and wheat for the baking of bread. There were tins of lard and the cleaning materials were loaded.

I took the bull horn and called out to all three ships and their response was that they were not ready to leave port yet---Not yet!---Not yet!

I pulled my chair from my cabin ad sat and continued to enjoy my pipes. I loved those Cuban cigars, but I saved them for special occasions.

While resting in my easy chair in front of my cabin, Officer O'Day came to me and said, "Sir, there are a number of seamen from other ships with various skills that are asking if you have a place for them on your ship with wages." I said, "Officer O'Day, yes, maybe we might. Are there any cooks?" O'Day said, "Yes Sir! There are two or three that know about barbeque. We have two Chinese who can cook their kinds of food. I have three cooks from an eatery called the "Fish House" who would like a job." I said, "Hire them all! We can use cooks on this long voyage. Anyone else down there?" O'Day said, "We have several who have worked at American gun shops. They look like us but don't talk like us."

I said, "Well, let's take them on and give them to the Gunnery Master. Are there any seamen with any sailing ship experience?" O'Day said, "Yes, a few that worked on two or one-masted ships." I said, "How many are there?" He said, "Twenty-three." I said, "Hire them and give them to the Sail Master. Is there anyone of higher ranking with higher skills?" The officer said, "Yes, there is one older man with navigational skills. He made it to shore after a pirate ship had downed his fighting ship." I said, "I want that man. I want to talk to him." O'Day said, "Alright Sir, but me must be at least thirty years old." I said, "So am I…So is Captain John, so bring him aboard. We officers, commanders and captains seem to grow older faster than most people!"

It was thirty minutes later when that sturdy, handsome navigator stood in front of us. He looked worn. I said, "Could you navigate a four-masted ship?" He said "No problem Sir! I have learned how to navigate by maps, currents, wind directions and the stars. That, with a good sail-master and helmsman, comes navigational experience after so many years. Sir, do you have a need for me or not?" I said, "What is your name navigator?" He said, "My name is Gottliep. It's German Sir!" I said, "Well, if you are my navigator, you have got to be a lieutenant. I am making you a Third Lieutenant with lieutenants pay which is considerable. You will join forces with my other navigator and share the work and teach one another a thing or two. You'll speak to me only when absolutely necessary. If I had everyone free to come to me to speak it would be annoying and time consuming."

I ordered that the First Navigator put Gottliep in a small cabin and gave him a cot and all the other information he would need.

Alone at last, I sat back and said, "Please, no more interruptions." Suddenly I heard a large shop right on the boardwalk adjacent to my ship. A man had just shot his mule in the head and there the mule was fully down in his harness. I said, "Why?" The man said, "He could not move. Not even when I hit him with a wooden plank would he move. That's what I get for buying a stubborn cheap donkey to pull my cart!"

I said to myself, "Please let that be all for a while." I snoozed in my chair for several hours.

I was resting soundly when I felt a hand shake my shoulder. I jumped straight up and faced Lieutenant Beatman. I looked straight down into his eyes, grimaced and said in a very loud, stern voice, "Never touch me while I am sleeping. You are lucky that you didn't feel my dagger. You may call to me loudly if necessary, to get my attention. Now step five paces backward and speak what is on your mind."

Beatman said, "I am sorry Sir, I wish to report that I checked with all of your Masters and Captains and they agree that everyone and everything is on board and waiting for further orders."

I sent word back to them by First Lieutenant Beatman that they will delay activities, take a ration of rum and eat, sleep and rest until they see the first sign of dawn. Then I will give further orders.

I did not say that I would say "Anchors Away!" For I know not what the night might bring.
I said, "Hold on Lieutenant. I want a few of my warrior seamen on each ship standing along side by the dock and tell them to give a warning shot if there is any sign of trouble. They should patrol the dock by walking back and forth to cover the area in front of our ships. Now be off with you. I am having my rum. My supper was brought to Annabelle and I, and we are going to eat and retire for the evening.

Annabelle and I were up at first light when we saw some orange lights on the horizon. I quickly shaved and dressed in my well-pressed commander's coat. I headed out of the cabin doors to take up the bull horn and called "Anchors Away!" My captains and crew were ready.

Good old Beatman, my First Lieutenant, for he had the crew ready and was the first to raise anchor. I called for minimum sails. All of the Sails Masters complied. My Sail Master adjusted the sails to catch the easterly wind, what there was of it. Our ships were released from their moorings and we crawled westward toward the St. Louis harbor entrance. No surprises...Good!

I led the way with Captain Beatman at the helm. The merchant ship followed me and Captain John trailed in his beautiful Spanish four-masted warship. He had twenty more cannons than I, so it took a little more wind to move that heavy ship. The Sail Master provided that by giving more sail. It was probably ten or fifteen minutes before we sailed our ship into the Mississippi.

Hellman, the Sail Master, adjusted our sails to catch a North wind as we headed South. Indeed, I ordered half-sails to move along more quickly. Dawn was barely upon us so we had to use extra care in not hitting something or grounding ourselves.

I heard several cannon shots coming from the shore. It was dark and they luckily missed. They were probably cannon placements to sink any ships on the Mississippi River. I think it was cannon fire from the pirate ships.
Soon we were again sailing east with sails adjusted to catch the winds. How I wish I could be at full-sail. But, with that merchant ship poking along, we could do no better in making time going westward.

I cut short the adventure. I had planned to sail along the Texas and Mexican coasts. There would be no interesting places we could harbor and I could tell in looking West there were black storm clouds full of lightening and thunder. The storm was heading our way. I hoped it would spend itself before reaching us. Wouldn't you know, that blast of wind and rain caught up with us and like it or not, we were being pushed eastward under high seas from the Gulf.

We managed to turn into the Cuban port and anchor to sit out the storm. The seamen that wanted to get off at Cuba were ready. The ten seamen needed two skiffs to make shore in the Cuban port. I sent my Third Lieutenant Gutfeld on one skiff and Officer Mueller on the other skiff to sail them to Havana's port. I had them hold fast before sailing because of a torrent of rain and wind. The Sail Master and seamen trained in sails already started lowering all sails to avoid sail damage and unnecessary movement of the ship. I said, "So, Lieutenant Gutfeld, when you and Officer Mueller check with the Sails Master, please pass the word along the waterfront that are looking for ten people who would be good single experienced crewmen. Tell them we will pay double the crewmen's wages, but do not show up unless you really have some years of experience on two or three-masted sailing ships."

In the next thirty minutes the storm was over. Only a little West wind remained. I said, "Okay, skiffs, on with you. Thank you for your service seamen. I know you have been paid before leaving! God bless you and have a great life!"

Our ship sat quietly in the water waiting for the return of our skiffs and hopefully with new experienced seamen aboard. My officers and lieutenants checked the ships for damages. I ordered that everyone eat heartily because it would be late evening before the galley would be serving supper.

It was nearly high noon before Lieutenant Gutfeld and Officer Mueller returned to the ship with a cargo of ten new seamen. My lieutenant took the job of assigning each crewman to the job for which they were most trained. Each new single crewman was given a side arm and would be paid according to their skill and level of experience. When that was done, I said, "Raise sails to half-mast and then weigh anchor!" Once again, we were leading my ships out to sea. We kept as much distance as we could as we sailed past Jamaica, Haiti and Puerto Rico, because their islands were pretty much taken over by pirates. I directed that we sail North until we found a large port in a city.

I kept Booker T. T. Masters next to me during the sail because he was so well studied in the Eastern American shores. Occasionally, I would say, "Booker, this looks like a good bay to turn into." He would say, "No, go on Sir!" And after a few hours, I said, "Booker, lets enter the Delaware Bay and go up the Delaware River to Philadelphia. We know what's facing the colonies from the British, but right now they can only expect punishment since the colonies are or about to revolt against their protectorant of Britain.

I asked Captain John to leave his best lieutenant at the helm and that he should join me aboard the Annabelle, and he did so by a small boat.

We rose the white flag at the top of each mast on all three ships and cautiously entered the Delaware River going North under quarter sails. All seamen in all positions including the cannoneers, were to assume readiness. All the way up the river Captain John and I used our bull horns and one after another we called, "We are friends and want to help!" As we neared Philadelphia, we saw many minutemen along the river poised to fire if we indicated that we were seeking reprisal for the revolt against the British Crown.
A small boat was sent to our mooring place along the Philadelphia docks. Captain John and Captain Booker joined me and we used the ships rope ladder to climb onto the dock. No sooner than we had stepped on the dock when the leader said, "We are minutemen fighting for our independence. Who are you?" I had never seen so many musket barrels pointed at us. I said, "We are three seamen---A Commander, a Captain and a Scholar---who are here to support your many needs. We have one thousand muskets and seven hundred pistols and a fortune in silver and gold to present to your cause, but only after we speak to your leader. Don't start thinking of taking our ships, because there are forty loaded cannons ready to blow you off the face of the earth if you try to board our ships. Even now, with a snap of our fingers, there are many muskets ready to drop you dead to the ground. So, take me to your leader where I can make this grand proposal which could win your war with British soldiers that will soon be coming to your shores." The minutemen

leader said, "Why would you want to help?" I said, "Because we do not believe in the British cause of starving you from your independence. We have many Irish and English friends who have come to these colonies for freedom, to enjoy their choice of religion and escape over taxation. I am British, but will not fight with my own warship. I will only help you defend your cause. You can do your fighting!"

The group cheered and said, "You said the right thing. We will now take you to Independence Hall where the leaders of the states are now meeting." I left my lieutenants with the biggest responsibility that they will ever have in their entire life time, with fortunes of silver and gold bars tucked away in the recesses of our ships. I called to the lieutenants, "Tie two cases of Jamaican rum on ropes and lower them!" The minutemen said, "What is that?" I said, "That is your entertainment for you and your leaders this night and many more to come. Strap the weight of them onto your horses and let's be on the way."

I said, "I am now confident in that you are who you say you are minutemen, therefore, find two large sturdy wagons and bring them to the side of Captain O'Day's merchant ship. I will have thirty of my one hundred warrior seamen lower the themselves to the ground level. They will wait until you find your wagons. Perhaps you should bring three wagons and line them up next to the loading platform by the merchant ship." Everyone watched impatiently until the horse drawn wagons were in line and ready to receive their offering. My warrior seamen brought one thousand muskets for them to load. They also brought seven hundred pistols. Along with those muskets, cases of musket balls and powder for all weapons were delivered. I said, "There will be a lot, so take off those shirts minutemen and put some muscle into it. I am glad your wagons each have their two horses to pull that load. Now minutemen, bring your wagons to the side of my ship and we will lower to you by ropes and pulleys just two cases of silver and gold. All of this should assure you and your leaders that we are sympathetic to your cause and willing to place a fortune where it will do the most good."

I stood at the helm and watched the minutemen work to load everything. The minutemen have now doubled in numbers. A leader of their squad called up to me and said, "We have three fine horses for you to ride to our Philadelphia Liberty Hall." Within minutes, we were on our way. We were all allowed to lead the procession of minutemen and wagons.

The wagons were hitched to posts directly in front of Liberty Hall. At some point along the way the wagons were covered with canvas so no English soldiers or nosey persons would know the wagons contents. I said to the minutemen leader, "Pass the word to every minuteman that if they reveal information about the contents of the wagons, they could cause an attack by the British soldiers. I am glad that you loaded hay atop of the wagons to further avert attention."

The minutemen stood guard. The meeting room doors were left slightly ajar. We sat outside the doors and listened to the representatives from all of the colonies arguing for and against trying for independence and the dangers of trying to secure their independence.

They continued to vote for and against fighting for independence with John Adams, Ben Franklin and Thomas Jefferson as well. Some representatives were afraid of the repercussions for losing to Britain. If they were defeated, they would be hung. Others said they did not mind paying taxes and liked being protected by England. These men represented the wealthy leaders and could pay the high taxes for sugar, tea and other things.

We three were led to the exterior room adjacent to the Congressional Chamber. The thin man Booker T. T. Masters said, "Sir, I have things to say when we enter these chambers." I said, "Mr. Thin Man, you may do just that!" I signaled to the lead minuteman to poke his head in the door and say, "There are men here who can provide a fortune in arms and weapons for your struggle for independence, as well as good advice. Are they welcome?" John Adams said, "Absolutely! By all means, we welcome them." I made my six-foot, six-inch frame as tall as I could and entered in British uniform. They were shocked. Along with me, I had six-foot, nine-inch Booker T. T. Masters and Captain John adding their presence to create a profound impression.

I said, "We have heard your needs for revolution, both pro and con. We can supply both arms and cash. You may all go to the window and look down to the street. You will see three wagons hitched to posts and covered with hay. We have on the first wagon, one thousand musket rifles with bayonets. On the next wagon, we have seven hundred pistols and as many swords and daggers. Also, on that wagon there are cases of musket balls and powder. Now, on the third wagon, I am bringing to you only one of the many chests of silver and gold that we will transfer to you through your minutemen. That one chest is full of gold coins. It is worth a fortune." All the congressmen from their states turned swiftly and applauded and said, "You are British. Why are you not using your ships to support your own British ships." I said, "The reason is that their cause is impure and selfish and immoral."

The Thin Man stepped in front of me and said, "I read Tom Payne and he was right. I read Thomas Jefferson and he was right. I read Ben Franklin. He had all the reasons why we should not be under the thumb of the British rule. The southern leaders of your states will lose all control if the northern states were to lose this battle. Mr. Franklin states that there are two million people living in the colonies that are paying too high taxes. There are ten million British who pay too little taxes. I heard just moments ago that there was a plan to write a Declaration of Independence. I say, God Bless those of you who sign it."

John Adams said, "We will write you a letter of commendation for what you have done today. You may have given us a better chance to win this Revolutionary War." I said, "Please Sir, do not write such a letter. If such a letter is seen, it will be a death warrant for us and we will hang as British turncoats. This meeting never happened Sir! I say the same to all of you Senators. You do not know us! We have done nothing for you! We have never been here!"

Captain John said, "We will leave these chambers while you men control the destiny of your country and all those living in it. Contact us on our warship, which is anchored on the Delaware River. Be sure that those accepting the fortune for your needs are honest and will be well-escorted back to wherever it is you keep your war funds.

As quickly as possible, have your trusted leaders box muskets and pistols with enough powder and balls to supply six weapons per box. Place these boxes with your revolution leaders on the farms adjacent to where you support your fighters so that you can easily retrieve them when war is upon you. Place boxes in pig pens, in cow barns with cow dung all around them, in horse barns with hay and manure! Place them in privies and in hay stalls, and everywhere that you believe a cannon soldier would not care to look! One of the first things the British will do when they come to your shores is to seek out any weapons you may have hidden away. We are only giving you a basic amount of arms but we are giving you over three million dollars to purchase more or have more made. Now we leave"

We hurried to our beautiful horses that we commandeered and headed to our warships and suddenly just before we left, John Adams spoke up and said, "Where did you get this fortune?" I said, "From a lifetime of commandeering privateers and Spanish warships. Now I am offering you the same. My credo has always been that money belongs to those who are most in need of it. Just before we leave gentlemen, your minutemen were very polite and orderly, so I wish them to join you in these chambers with two cases of hard-to-get Jamaican rum." I saw Ben Franklin nearly fall from his chair when he heard such news. I said, "These are fine horses. My Captain Harris breeds horses, so I may just keep them. We certainly paid enough for them."

After we left Liberty Hall, we got on our horses and three British officers on their fancy steeds galloped up to us and said, "You are not allowed to carry swords, pistols and daggers on our streets." I said, "These are not your streets. These are American streets." They said, "Now, either pull your weapons or keep moving." The officers could not resist the challenge. This was said by three lowly men on horseback. We each took one of the men. Naturally, I took my epee and slashed his right hand and gun belt off and grabbed his horse's reins and kicked the man off his saddle. He ran screaming like a stuck pig!

Captain John has a thing for shooting his opponents considerably below the belt! The English officer threw his pistol onto the ground and reached for his groin screaming. I was in a position where I could kick that man off his saddle and crab the reins of his horse. The Thin Man pulled his horse close to the British officer and raised his long legs and kicked him right below the chin so hard the man's teeth flew from his mouth. Thin Man also kicked the British do-gooder off his saddle and grabbed the horse's bridle.

Now, here we are with six horses. We were riding three and holding three. This was going to make Aaron very happy when he sees that he can add six more horses to his stables on board the merchant ship. It was really late in the day when we presented my brother-in-law Aaron with the horses. The first three horses were bred for trotting and we weren't sure about the other three. Aaron will have to tell us.

It was an interesting ride back to our ships after that incident. As we left off for our ships, we gained the attention of other British police and they came galloping towards us. As we neared our ships, our musketeers were ready as they always were and they sent off a volley of shots at the red-coated British police on mounts. They quickly retreated. I thanked my sharp shooters with a wave and they waved back. Many of the British were hit in one place or another on their bodies and it should be some time before they will be fighting against their American revolutionaries.

Captain John boarded his own ship by rope ladder and I did the same. I said, "What a day this has been!"

I was looking at our docking situation and wondered how I was going to turn our ships down river since the Delaware was so narrow at this point on the river. I said, "Sails Master, continue to try to sail and make adjustments to get our ships moving backwards down-stream."

We three watched more sails adjustments than ever I knew were possible and still our ships moved East and West, then a little right, then a little left…nothing! After watching this for awhile I said, "My conclusion is the four-masted warship cannot sail in reverse." I knew that everyone who observed what I was about to have done would think it humorous, and it would become a story to be repeated.

I called to Captain O'Day on the horn, "Sail your vessel to the stern of my ship." He replied, "Aye, Sir! How far away from your stern should I be?" I said, "We will try fifteen yards. Hold that position. Lieutenant, pass those heavy mooring ropes to Captain O'Day and tie the other end to our mooring posts." I then went to the bow of the boat and said, "Captain John, work your way closer somehow to the bow of the Annabelle. If you can, back your stern to within twenty yards of my bow. Cast your mooring line onto my ship. We will secure these lines to a mooring post on our bow." I said, "Captain, now this will be a first that you can tell stories about. We are about to be pulled backwards by a small merchant ship. If he can…"

I called out, "Lower sails!" and the Sails Masters on both ships complied. I went back to the stern and said, "Captain O'Day, put these sails fully open and catch the North Delaware winds and move us out into mid-stream." It was like walking in a dream, where you walk and don't move. I could feel that indeed, we were moving. As we journeyed mid-stream, we felt the current helping us move along. I called to Captain O'Day and said, "Good job! Keep us moving until we reach a point wide enough so that we may turn our ships to the South."

We were elated. Within two hours Captain O'Day took his place between our two warships and we sailed with some speed. All of those along the shores of the Delaware would be called liars if they were to try to convince anyone that they saw massive warships sailing in reverse. They would not have seen the tow ropes involved I that strange occasion. At last we sailed into the Delaware Bay. I gave word by horn that we were going to sail South to the Atlantic to avoid meeting any of the English warships bound for the colonies. We would, however, probably face a pirate ship in the southern-most part of the Mid-Atlantic.

I can't believe our good fortune. As we sailed South, we identified two Spanish ships. One that was carrying a treasure fortune. It had no cannons, but it did have an escort of another Spanish vessel. I said to my teacher, "Captain Thin Man, I think the Spanish felt that they could move their treasure ship to the West because the English warships were tantamount on reclaiming the colonies."

All cannoneers on the Annabelle fired a volley of twenty cannon shots to the main masts. The masts came tumbling down! I did not even have to use my long cannons at the bow of the Annabelle. Up popped their white flag signifying their defeat.

Captain John did not see the white flags or did not believe them for he sent another volley of twenty cannon blasts to the deck of that ship. He was right because now they were firing their cannons at us from both sides of their decks. I said, "We could be hurt! Sails Master Hellman, back off!" And we did so swiftly to a reasonable distance so their cannon fire could not reach us but ours could reach them.

Captain John did not have that capability with special cannons so he navigated to the rear of that massive Spanish ship where their heavy cannons could not directly fire at him. The angle was of out of reach.

I knew the Spanish Captain and crew were waiting for the cannon blasts that would sink them. Yes, and that is exactly what happened. I reloaded my leeward cannons and sent twenty cannons into the side of that poor ship. The enemy cannoneers met their death. Captain John was now able to put his twenty cannons on the port side of that massive Spanish ship. He did! There were explosions and there was fire and there was sadness. We won another battle at sea at the cost many brave seamen.

The captain of that Spanish galleon still lived. He came to his helm under the lights of fire, raising his arms in the air and saying a prayer or signal of consignment of his death. We would not know because we quickly commandeered that treasure ship. We quickly secured tow ropes. The seas were fairly smooth and I sent two of my small boats towards the treasure ship. A few of my warrior seamen were o both oats. I had several of my warrior seamen strap themselves to the lower yardarms of the Annabelle where they could see any enemy seamen that could be raising a musket. Indeed, they were and my musketeers polished them off one-by-one as they rose their hands to fire. Captain John was doing the same with his warrior crewmen.

We maintained that logistical advantage for several hours until there was absolutely no sign of movement. I called out to the small boats, "Board that treasure ship but be ready with pistols for anyone that they may be playing possum. If you are not sure, shoot it anyway. I do not want one of you to be injured." The crewmen of my small boats made their way up the rope ladder of that treasure ship and stayed in position with crewmen from Captain John's small boats. They climbed the rope ladder on the opposite side of the treasure ship. During that time under the glare of the burning Spanish ships, we still waited. We knew that there were more men aboard that treasure ship that did not show themselves earlier. They had to be hiding on the lower deck of this treasure ship. I ordered everyone to "hold fast" until dawn and then we will ferret out these rascals. They too will be tired, afraid, hungry and thirsty.

We waited till the sun had risen to where there was ample light to discover the hideaway of the remaining crewmen of the treasure ship that were giving their lives to protect.

Soon I heard a shot and then another…and then another, and then another and then another…until we finally heard the Spanish words "We give up!" I said in Spanish, "Show yourselves one-by-one!" They did. They crept from the bowels of that treasure ship holding their weapons. Of course, they dropped all of their weapons and word was sent, "Do not enter the deck with a weapon or you will be shot!" It took about an hour for forty of those miserable Spanish devils to give up! To each one we said, "Your Master Warship is not sunk, so leap into the ocean and crawl aboard your Spanish Galleon." What I thought to be forty jumping into the water one-by-one turned out to be sixty on that ship. What a surprise!

We examined every crewman and cannoneers on board the ship. We removed the dead and the one living and pushed them all overboard. I said, "Cannoneers, stay…plant a cannonball onto the rudder and one more into their helm and cannoneer Willie, fire a cannonball into where you think they store their cannon powder. It was a good guess and there was a mighty explosion. Now cannoneers, put a broadside cannon directly at the cannon ports…both upper and lower on both sides of their ship. Now put under tow this wonderful treasure ship that will bring us new wealth for our adventures to come."

We drew away swiftly from the fiery ship. I looked back to see that Captain John had their ship in tow. We pulled away from the other ship's burning ashes on the sea. I had ordered that all cannons from both ships be loaded and ready to fire because we were susceptible going through these pirate waters. I prayed there would be no disturbances to our sails to Ireland and England.

With Spanish flags on our masts, I felt fairly safe that we would not be accosted by any ship bearing a Spanish flag. I know that some of the Spanish captains would be wondering why we had one of our treasure ships in tow. I would wonder too!

It was so confusing to them that they went about their other assigned missions. I am glad it was still night time or they could probably see the truth of it. It was nearly dawn when we saw the southwestern area of Spain. I said, "Change flags back to the English flags!" We turned North by Northeast directly towards Ireland. The channel crossing took only two hours under half-sail. We entered the Irish Sea into that memorable Irish Bay where we had first commandeered two Spanish ships some years ago. We anchored in that harbor and loaded up all the seamen who wished to stay with their families that they had left. We loaded them with silver and gold coin and said, "Don't forget us for we will not have forgotten you. You may again ride the waves on the Annabelle with your Commander Joseph Worthy."

They were thrilled in mooring on the island under the direction of Captain Gottliep. The departure of these excellent seamen had dwindled our required numbers to fewer men than I was comfortable in sailing my ship. We made haste as soon as Captain Gottliep returned. While we were here, I could hear Mickey O'Hara screaming, "We don't leave here without loading up with cases of Irish Whiskey. We will need all we can get to create a new Bounty Pub!"

Well, here we are again sending word out. Six of our skiffs from two ships were sent to the harbor. Words do travel. We were needing to buy all the cases of Irish Whiskey that were available. It came by wagon, carriage or by hand all the cases of Irish Whiskey our skiffs could hold.

It was a quick turn-around. After all was loaded, the skiffs were tied to our warships. We made a beeline to the Annabelle Harbor. What a beautiful sight that was as we sailed into the harbor. We sent word by our small boats to the Harbor Master to clear all mooring stations and all the docks for Captain Worthy has returned along with his crews and ships. Of course, we sent ample coin to the Harbor Master who shared it with the ships he had to move out.

Our two warships sidled up to the dock and moored our ships in place. Captain O'Day said, "How about me, Sir?" I said, "You do exactly what Mr. Aaron O'Hara tells you to do. He will supply you with sufficient coin to do as he says and we will secure a mooring place near wherever he tells you to go. I know where that would be, at least I thought I did. Now for the magic of the treasure ship. I had it moored on the dock between Captain John's warship and my own warship. No one was allowed on that ship until morning.

I had posted four warrior seamen to guard that ship with their lives and warned everyone to stay away. Captain John and I went to the boarding ramp of that Spanish treasure ship with lots of guns. We looked at one another and smiled. I said, "Shall we, Captain John?" We boarded and looked into the cabins. There was nothing there. Next, we took and lit our gas lanterns going to the door of the stairwell. We took the dozen steps down the stairway to the second deck. There were stacks of kegs on either side of the ship's walls, both fore and aft where the cannons were placed. I said, "What a way to hide gold and silver, Captain John." He laughed. We grabbed a hatchet from the door of the storage room. I said, "Do me the honor Captain John, break that barrel open and let that beautiful coin spill out of the kegs." He took three major hatchet blows to the topo and side of the keg. Our smiles disappeared in a second for what came spewing out from these kegs were nails for building ships or homes. I said, "Quickly, try a few more of these kegs, Captain John!" He did…all nails! "You know, these are all hand-hewn nails---very expensive. The nails are a tremendous find for us." There were also a few new items I had heard about called screws. We laughed and said, "It's a good thing our future is not depending on this. What a surprise! Let's go to this third deck and see what's there."

I said, "Oh yes! There are chests stacked along all of the walls from fore to aft." Captain John gently knocked the lock on this first of many chests and opened it gently as you would a hand of poker cards. In one word we said together, "Eureka!" Again, we have built our wealth up to a massive fortune. And it was as much as what we started with on our adventures at sea. I immediately called the pay master and lieutenants to come take a look and said, "See how much money we are going to share. Now our pay master and our accountant will stay here and count this fortune. Captain John and I will go to the top deck where we will be waiting for the good news." Of course, Booker T. T. Masters joined the team to insure the math was right. He is, after all, a teacher, master, and professional and our conscience on may things.

We all sat on separate barrels of rum. I said, "Captain, shall we?" He said, "We shall!" We brought out two large steins and opened the barrel's spigot and filled those steins. I said, "We will give some to our workers on the lower deck just as soon as they are finished counting our money." We sat and waited at least three hours before they came to us on top deck. "As you thought Captain, it is a massive fortune. A King's ransom twice over!" We all agreed to place that money where it would do the most good, where we could. We knew that we could not individually spend it in a lifetime.

The next morning. I ordered the pay master to calculate how much we owed to each of our crewmen and give special bonuses to all members of our warrior seamen. I said, "Officers and lieutenants, don't forget to count your bonuses as well! Each of you lieutenants may now release all seamen to join their families."

The crewmen put their fortune in small leather satchels and went home. I said, "They will have one month to make a decision if they want to return to sea duty. It will be as before. We will protect the eastern shores of Ireland and the western shores of England. We will not engage in battle unless we are challenged. As you know, I have one single-masted ship to give to our Irish crewmen who wish to cross the Irish Sea and moor at a port of their choice."

We had fifteen Irish crewmen that took their fortune in coin and went to that one-masted boat at the end of the boardwalk where it was moored. I asked, "Who will sail it for them? Is there one officer among you Irish seamen that can sail a boat? Can you navigate your way across the Irish Sea?" They said, "Not sure Captain!" I said, "Now you have a problem, don't you?" Then one of the remaining crewmen called out and said, "Do you remember me Sir? I have been learning to navigate for the past two years. I am single and would love to go to Ireland and meet a pretty Irish lass and I might even wed." I said, "Pay master, give that young navigator his wages. Don't forget your belongings and be off with you!"

Captain John looked at me and said, "Looks like we have a lot of renovating to do on this captured treasure ship." I said, "Yes we do, Captain John. But soon you are to lose your warship." Captain John paled in hearing that. I said, "Come to my cabin, rest, have a cigar and a glass of Irish Whiskey while I smoke my favorite pipe and join you in a drink. Do you remember when we commandeered that forty-cannon, beautiful Spanish warship that belonged to the King of Spain?" Captain John said, "Yes, I remember and now I remember it was your plan to bring this magnificent ship back to England and place it where the old burned down Bounty Pub used to be."

I said, "You are right Captain John. That will take some work. You and your other two captains, and your officers as well as my own, are to hire workers to clear that rubble that was a great pub. When that area is clear, I want to contract with a company to build a maritime building to sit where the Bounty use to sit. This is where the pay master will have his new office.

All ships entering and leaving the Annabelle harbor will register their destination and their cargo, their captains, and other lieutenants and officers and all the crewmen. I will staff the second level of the Maritime building. The owners of all ships will make known the ship or ships that they own. I will have many insurance agents ready to sell the life insurance in amounts that will match the value of their cargo. They must insure all those sailing on their ships in an amount coinciding with their position and experience. You will have ample profits to do this for you will be selling to different countries and buying cargo from other countries to return to England or any other port you so designate. You will also pay fair taxes to the Crown based on a percentage of profits. They can negotiate with the tax man. I will ask the Admiral to provide warship protection on their journeys."

I said, "Captain John, you will leave your magnificent four-masted Spanish warship right where it sits along side the boardwalk. It will be chained to several heavy-duty iron posts that are placed both on the dock and the outer edge of the boardwalk. The chains, as well as the metal mooring posts, will be covered in gold leaf.

You will lower all canvas and Aaron, the new manager, will have them raised only on special occasions. Just like the Bounty, we will create a heavy-duty off-ramp leading down to the boardwalk. We will place an under-plank to allow for the movement of this ship caused by wind and water. You will please, Captain John, take charge of this project and I will repay you many times over. Do not forget at least two tons of heavy ballast rock will be delivered to the third deck, both bow and stern. This ballast rock will add stability to prevent too much movement on the water and along the dock's edge. You may stay with your family during this project.

I want every bar varnished and double polished on the outside and the inside of this highly decorated ship. Hire a smelter to melt down gold and create the gold leaf that you are going to use on all the carvings throughout the ship.

As soon as my brother-in-law Aaron determines what to do with his thoroughbreds during this renovation, he will come back and help you. My wife, Annabelle, will help you as well. She will insist on laying out the entertaining deck with the stage and bars and storage area for rum, whiskey and beer. I expect that within a year this ship will be the hit of London. Buy, demolish and clear the adjacent building next to the

Maritime building on the boardwalk and put hitching posts for the many horses and carriages that will soon be hitched there.

Now, Sir, we are going to take that one hundred twenty-gun treasure ship which is well built but has suffered some damage and deliver it to the shipyard. I will personally take that ship to the best English warship shipyard and have its sails refurbished like mine and have the four masts replaced with new sails. In the renovation everything that looks old will be replaced with new. You may even have new rudders. Whatever you wish to include by way of comfort or safety additions or enhancements, you may order it to be built. You will even have gold leaf letters inscribed on its hull. While the new Maritime building is being built, your new ship will be undergoing transformation to a fighting sea warship. If you have any changes or additions to your ship, you will have to have Captain O'Day take you to the ship yards with your special requests. Maybe you would like bigger or more cabins, or maybe you would like steel plates added where it would protect your powder room and your cabin and along the waterline of both sides of your warship."

Captain John said, "Joseph, these are grand ideas and I would be proud to sail such a vessel with you in protecting the shores on the eastern side of Ireland and the western shores of England. I know that the kind of ship that you are building for me will be very expensive." I said, "Captain John, you are worth it. Now as we secure the waters of Ireland and England, you will have the might and I will have the flexibility. I would rather have these ships and not need them than need the ships and not have them."

Suddenly, there was a rapping at my cabin door and in came my brother-in-law Aaron. I said, "Tell me about it, Aaron. What did you do with your thoroughbred horses?" Aaron said, "I bought one-half interest in the largest racing stables in England. I have contracted with groomers and trainers and a feed lot to provide all the needs of my three trotters, twelve racing thoroughbreds and the other three that look totally out of place. I have written a contract with General Nicholby to race his horses and my horses equally and we will share in the winnings. The General is used to doing this and I believe that this is his hobby rather than a source of income. We agreed to breed his winners and my winners with the best racing stallions that we could find. So, Captain, I am now free to help re-establish a home with my family near the new Bounty Pub."

I said, "Good, you are going to be very busy. I wish for you to assist Captain John in re-furbishing the new Bounty. Aaron, as before, you will manage the beverage, sales and inventory. Annabelle will have directed the building of a new and bigger stage and I will interview, manage and schedule entertainers as we did before. My Annabelle says she will play the spinet and sing, but chooses not to dancer. When this project nears completion, we will have Captain O'Day take her to Ireland to bring back a young group of singers, dancers and musicians just like before. Until then, let's ask how you wish Captain John to build the bar, storage area and anything else you might need to make the new Bounty twice the size and beauty of the old one. You may use gold leaf on the bar and the gas lanterns and on anything else you want."

I said, "Aaron, you should know, I will be busy building a bank adjacent to the Maritime building. You must know you have a fortune that you have accumulated that will go into that bank and be under your control. This bank will be twice the size of the bank I built in Cuba. While your Bounty and Captain John's ship are being built, so will the bank. There will be a below ground large area walled in steel. The ceiling will also be of steel. The floor will be of steel. Across the front of this ironed in vault, I will have heavy duty iron bars extend the full width and length of our impenetrable vault. This vault has to be large to accommodate the many chests of silver and gold that we have stored in my ship and Captain John's ship which is now going to be the Bounty. An iron door will be installed in front of a cage. It will have three keys---one for the bank manager, one for the pay master and one for me. Guess who will be the bank manager? Of course, Mikey O'Hara will qualify. He is the most trustworthy man I will ever know. What Mr. O'Hara does not know about banking, he will hire the people who do know.

If anyone is seen on this level of the bank, they will either be shot or placed in the Milford jail. As soon as the construction is completed on the two levels and the banking service areas are completed, I want all gold and silver coin and bars moved from my ship to that bank vault.

Security guards will be placed outside of the bank for twenty-four hours a day, seven days a week. There will be a roof constructed under which they may stand. I will hire a construction company from London to build this bank according to their knowledge of how a bank should be built. They will also adhere to my instructions in building a special area for inside security.

For now, I want all the gold on that treasure ship to be moved to the lower deck of the Annabelle. I will have fifty warrior seamen guard the outside and inside of that ship and that group will be managed by Booker T. T. Masters. As soon as the captain moored, I ordered all gold be stored on the Annabelle because that beautiful Spanish ship is going to be the new Bounty.

I will sail that wonderful treasure ship to the shipyards in a few days. Patch it up the best you can. I will have my sail master put together a sail rigging that will get us there. I will be staying at the shipyards for a while. Annabelle has bought a comfortable home about two hundred yards from the boardwalk within the area of the new Bounty Pub. Her mother Anne and Mickey will live in a nice home being built adjacent to my own. They will be able to take care of my child."

I said, "Captain John, I want you and your family to lease the best space available in our Milford Hotel while you have a home built for you in any place you desire. Start your new assignments. I want you to think of nothing except for work…seven days a week, except for Sundays… until we meet our objectives."

It has been a year since all these activities started and I have nothing new to report. I will not try to detail the rigors of all the work that was done during the last eighteen months. The Bounty is completed and already doing business. The crewmen are filling the jobs provided for them. Captain John's new one hundred twenty-gun warship is along side of my Annabelle warship and moored to the dock. Captain John is in his new house and the children are attending school. My son, Will, is at school also. All the single entertainers doing singing and music are already performing. A huge hotel has been built near the new Bounty Pub. Mickey is the Bank Manager and Anne is managing the money. Every entertainer has a place to live that they can call their own. Captain O'Day has a thriving business moving both people and cargo to Irish and English shores."

I know you are asking, do we have that much wealth to be able to do all of this? My answer is, yes. In fact, Captain John and I want you to hire the men and provide the materials to build an extensive boardwalk up to one hundred yards. I want it twice as wide. This is where we would designate the part of loading and off-loading cargo from all ships. A manifest of that cargo from each ship will be presented to the harbor master officers before ships are loaded or off-loaded. This will support our new Maritime laws that I have personally written and ascribed to by myself and will present to the English Parliament for inclusion in the English Maritime Law.

I am delaying you from proceeding with these complex and difficult projects. I am sorry, so now I say be off with you. Resolve your problems if you can before coming to me.

I am comfortable in knowing that the seas are protected from pirates by my warship Annabelle and Captain John's gigantic one hundred twenty cannon warship. There must be something wrong in that I am not having complaints from anyone. It is a good place for me to say goodbye for now from all the Worthy family and the O'Hara family, Captain John and the magnificent Booker T. T. Masters.

Until the next read, God Bless you all!

EPILOGUE

This message to you both saddens and yet gladdens me. I am sad to report that I will no longer command my warship Annabelle in taking on new adventures on the high seas.

My young children, as well as the children of my other captains, are all in school. Even many of my seamen had decided to become land owners with their own families. It is hard to recruit young seamen with a twit of skill. So, your Commander Joseph and his foremost Captain John, are now family men destined to spend their lives on shore.

I am happy to announce that my son, Will Worthy, will now be the captain of my one-of-a-kind warship. He has been sailing with me for most of the time in the three books that I have just completed. He is strong, as tall as I, and fully trained in all the ship's positions. He has been on his own now for three years sailing the high seas and will report to you in the next book of all the weird and strange events of warship battle. He is, as you know, the fourth generation of Worthys. First it was Captain Eric, then Captain Alexander, my father---then myself, Commander Joseph Worthy and now my son, Will Worthy. Will Worthy will tell you of all these adventures in the fourth book called, "Captain Will Worthy's Warship Adventures" sailing my old warship.

I have taken the gold letters spelling Annabelle from both sides of my ship. It will be part of Annabelle's memory box. I have told Will he can put the name of his own woman, if he finds one, on the side of his ship.

It will be Will Worthy talking to you in first person in that fourth book. He has more strength and knowledge of the sea than I did at his age.

The new readers of my adventures will want to go back and read all three books to see what Will Worthy has been through.

By the way, the majestic Booker T. T. Masters will be at Will's side as he was by mine. A master in all weapons.

You will get a good look at all the adventures of my father-in-law Mickey and his wife Anne O'Hara as thay deal with the gamblers and the drinkers at the new Bounty Pub. My brother-in-law Aaron is in the book as well. There are a variety of adventures by all.

Good reading to you
Love from Annabelle and
Myself, Captain Joseph Worthy

Printed in the United States
By Bookmasters